Fuzzy Baseball

3

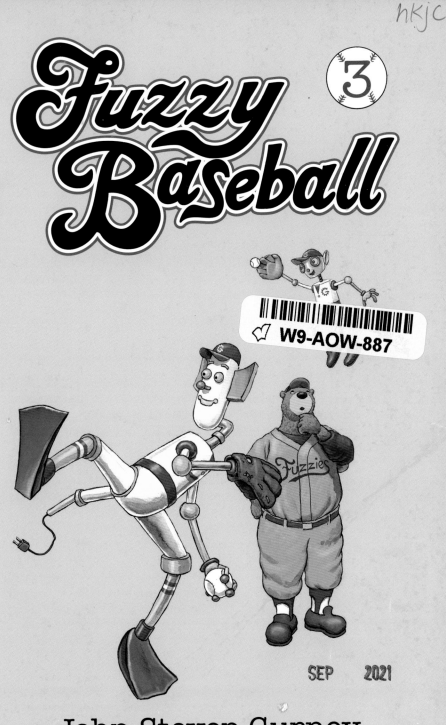

John Steven Gurney

PAPERCUTZ

To my buddy Leo, the Official Baseball Consultant for the
FUZZY BASEBALL Series. And to Kathie.

Fuzzy Baseball #3
"RBI Robots"
Created by JOHN STEVEN GURNEY
JAYJAY JACKSON—Production
JEFF WHITMAN—Managing Editor
JIM SALICRUP
Editor-in-Chief

FUZZY BASEBALL #3 "RBI Robots" © 2020
by John Steven Gurney.
All other material © 2020 by Papercutz.

Hardcover ISBN: 978-1-5458-0476-6
Paperback ISBN: 978-1-5458-0475-9

Printed in China
May 2019

Papercutz books may be purchased for
business or promotional use.
For information on bulk purchases please contact
Macmillan Corporate and Premium Sales Department at
(800) 221-795 x5442.

Distributed by Macmillan
First printing

INTRODUCING THE GEARTOWN CLANKEES...

ZZOOOSH

WELL, THEY LOOK LIKE REALLY GOOD BALLPLAYERS.

ONE BY ONE, THE CLANKEES TAKE OFF THEIR MASKS...

14

THE FUZZIES RETURN TO THE FIELD...

BILLY THE GROUNDSKEEPER

WE'LL JUST PLAY OUR BEST UNTIL THEY RUN OUT OF POWER.

HOW WILL WE KNOW?

I CAN HELP YOU WITH THAT.

MY ELECTRIC CLIPPER HAS A GREEN LIGHT. WHEN THE POWER IS LOW, THE LIGHT IS YELLOW.

WHEN THE POWER RUNS OUT, THE LIGHT IS RED.

ALL OF THOSE ROBOTS HAVE GREEN LIGHTS.

WHEN THEIR POWER IS LOW, THE LIGHTS WILL BE YELLOW. WHEN THEIR POWER IS GONE, THE LIGHTS WILL BE RED.

ONE OUT, RUNNER AT THIRD... THE NEXT BATTER IS *JOHNNY WRENCH.*

RED SEEMS TO BE SETTLING IN, HE STRIKES OUT JOHNNY...

HONUS IS TAKING A HUGE LEAD AT THIRD.

CRANK HITS IT DEEP...

CRACK

KAZUKI KOALA MAKES AN AMAZING CATCH FOR THE THIRD OUT...

IT'S THE BOTTOM OF THE FIRST INNING. PEPE PERRITO IS BATTING FOR THE FUZZIES...

I THINK THESE ROBOTS ARE OKAY.

I MUST DO SOMETHING!

26

29

43

SEVENTH INNING AND THE SCORE IS TIED AT 2 TO 2. NO OUTS, AND THE CLANKEES ARE UP...

LOOK, WE'RE JUST GOING TO SHOW YOU THE HIGHLIGHTS FROM THE NEXT COUPLE DOZEN INNINGS, OR ELSE THIS BOOK IS GOING TO BE LIKE 300 PAGES.

EIGHTH INNING: HONUS WINGNUT RUNS OUT OF POWER AND IS REPLACED BY **LOU GEARIG**...

NINTH INNING: WALTER WOMBAT STRIKES OUT AND SENDS THE GAME INTO EXTRA INNINGS...

STRIKE THREE!

OOPS!

TWELFTH INNING: **PERCIVALE PENGUINO** GOES IN FOR KAZUKI KOALA…

FIFTEENTH INNING: TECHY MATSUI RUNS OUT OF POWER AND IS REPLACED BY **HARMON KILOWATT**…

EIGHTEENTH INNING: PITCHING CHANGE, **KIT OCELOT** COMES IN FOR THE FUZZIES…

TWENTY-FIRST INNING: PITCHING CHANGE, **ROTOR HORNSBY** COMES IN FOR THE CLANKEES…

TWENTY-THIRD INNING: THE GAME IS STILL TIED AT 2…

TWENTY-SIXTH INNING: **CRUSTY FOB** GOES IN FOR TY COG…

OY VEY! THIS GAME IS GOING ON FOREVER. I'M GOING TO READ SOME MORE OF HAMMY'S BOOK. I'LL SKIP AHEAD A FEW PAGES.

IT'S THE BOTTOM OF THE THIRTY-EIGHTH INNING. TWO OUTS, NO ONE ON BASE, AND THE SCORE IS STILL 2 TO 2...

BLOSSOM STEPS UP TO THE PLATE...

ROTOR WINDS UP...

HERE'S THE PITCH...

60

THE BALL ROLLS TO A STOP BY AXEL ROD REGREASE...

BLOSSOM TIPTOES PAST FIRST AND HEADS FOR SECOND...

SHE ROUNDS SECOND AND HEADS FOR THIRD...

A MEMO FROM THE COMMISIONER

As I was writing this book I had a lot of fun coming up with the names for the Geartown Clankees. Although some of the Fuzzies are named after actual players (Jackie Robinson and Sammy Sosa) every one of the Clankees are named after players from baseball history. The challenge was to find names that I could blend with words associated with engines, robots, or anything mechanical. I imagine that adults will groan as they read my puns, but I hope young readers will be curious enough to look up some of these baseball greats. I should add that the positions the characters play in this book do not necessarily correspond with the positions that they played in real life.
Here is a list of the actual players:

Harmon Killebrew   Lou Gehrig   Johnny Bench   Rogers Hornsby
    Rusty Staub   Alex Rodriguez   Ty Cobb   Greg Luzinski
                Bucky Dent   Cy Young
                    Mark McGwire   Honus Wagner
                Kirby Puckett   Hank Aaron
                        Hideki Matsui

LEARN TO SPEAK ITALIAN WITH PERCIVALE PENGUINO

robot amichevoli – friendy robots

sfortuna – bad luck

posso giocare – I can play

THE FERNWOOD VALLEY FUZZIES

#1/8 Blossom Honey-Possum, Outfield
#7   Percivale Penguino, Outfield
#8   Pam the Lamb, Outfield
#10 Larry Boa, Third Base
#13 Pepe Perrito, Shortstop
#19 Kazuki Koala, Outfield
#21 Hammy Sosa, Catcher
#24 Pony Perez, Shortstop
#29 Red Kowasaki, Pitcher
#32 Sandy Kofox, Pitcher
#34 Bo Grizzly, First Base & Manager
#42 Jackie Rabbitson, Second Base
#44 Walter Wombat, Outfield
#45 Kit Ocelot, Pitcher

THE GEARTOWN CLANKEES

#3 Harmon Kilowatt, third base
#4 Lou Gearig, right field
#5 Johnny Wrench, catcher
#9 Rotor Hornsby, pitcher
#10 Crusty Fob, left field
#13 Axel Rod Regrease, shortstop
#15 Ty Cog, left field
#19 Greg Pluginsky, second base
#20 Clunky Dent, Manager
#24 Cyborg Young, pitcher
#25 Spark McPlyer, first base
#33 Honus Wingnut, right field
#34 Kirby Sprocket, pitcher
#44 Crank Aaron, center field
#55 Techy Matsui, third base

WATCH OUT FOR PAPERCUTZ™

Welcome to FUZZY BASEBALL #3 "RBI Robots" by John Steven Gurney, "The Commissioner," from Papercutz, those Fuzzy-fans in the cheap seats dedicated to publishing great graphic novels for all ages. I'm Jim Salicrup, Editor-in-Chief and former Assistant Coach for the Fernwood Valley Fuzzies. I'm really excited to announce that in addition to producing FUZZY BASEBALL graphic novels, as well as assembling all our other incredible graphic novels, we got some exciting exciting Papercutz publishing news—so exciting, it was even in the New York Times and The Hollywood Reporter! So exciting, I'm going to tell you all about it right now...

Papercutz has managed to get the North American rights to publish perhaps the most successful comics series in the world—ASTERIX! Now some of you may not have heard of this Asterix fella, so let's take a quick journey in the Papercutz time machine...

We're back in the year 50 BC in the ancient country of Gaul, located where France, Belgium, and the Southern Netherlands are today. All of Gaul has been conquered by the Romans... well, not all of it. One tiny village, inhabited by indomitable Gauls, resists the invaders again and again. That doesn't make it easy for the garrisons of Roman soldiers surrounding the village in fortified camps. So, how's it possible that a small village can hold its own against the mighty Roman Empire? The answer is this guy...

This is **Asterix**. A shrewd, little warrior of keen intellect... and superhuman strength. Asterix gets his superhuman strength from a magic potion. But he's not alone.

Obelix is Asterix's inseparable friend. He too has superhuman strength. He's a menhir (tall, upright stone monuments) deliveryman, he loves eating wild boar and getting into brawls. Obelix is always ready to drop everything to go off on a new adventure with Asterix.

Panoramix, the village's venerable Druid, gathers mistletoe and prepares magic potions. His greatest success is the power potion. When a villager drinks this magical elixir he or she is temporarily granted super-strength. This is just one of the Druid's potions! And now you know why this small village can survive, despite seemingly impossible odds. While we're here, we may as well meet a few other Gauls...

Cacofonix is the bard—the village poet. Opinions about his talents are divided: he thinks he's awesome, everybody else think he's awful, but when he doesn't say anything, he's a cheerful companion and well-liked...

Vitalstatistix, finally, is the village's chief. Majestic, courageous, and irritable, the old warrior is respected by his men and feared by his enemies. Vitalstatistix has only one fear: that the sky will fall on his head but, as he says himself, "That'll be the day!"

There are plenty more characters around here, but you've met enough for now. In other words, that's Gaul, folks! It's time we get back and wrap this up. Now, where did we put that time machine? Oh, there it is!

We're back, and we hope you enjoyed this trip back in time to explore 50 BC. For more information about ASTERIX and his upcoming Papercutz graphic novels, just go to papercutz.com. As for FUZZY BASEBALL, all we can say is, "Play Gaul—er, we mean BALL!"

Thanks,

Jim

STAY IN TOUCH!

EMAIL: salicrup@papercutz.com
WEB: papercutz.com
TWITTER: @papercutzgn
INSTAGRAM: @papercutzgn
FACEBOOK: PAPERCUTZGRAPHICNOVELS
REGULAR MAIL: Papercutz, 160 Broadway, Suite 700, East Wing, New York, NY 10038